Twenty-Minute Tales

Enid Blyton

Twenty-Minute Tales

A DRAGON BOOK

GRANADA
London Toronto Sydney New York

Published by Granada Publishing Limited in 1972
Reprinted 1974, 1976, 1977, 1979, 1981

ISBN 0 583 30165 7

First published by Methuen & Co Ltd 1940
Copyright © Enid Blyton 1940

Granada Publishing Limited
Frogmore, St Albans, Herts AL2 2NF
and
36 Golden Square, London W1R 4AH
866 United Nations Plaza, New York, NY 10017, USA
117 York Street, Sydney, NSW 2000, Australia
100 Skyway Avenue, Rexdale, Ontario, M9W 3A6, Canada
61 Beach Road, Auckland, New Zealand

Printed and bound in Great Britain by
Cox & Wyman Ltd, Reading
Set in Intertype Times

Contents

1: *Feefo, the Pixie Dog*

Feefo belonged to the King of Fairyland. He was a beautiful white dog, not very large, with lovely brown eyes and a tail that could wag faster than any other dog's in the land.

He was the only dog that the King kept, and he was very proud of himself. The Queen spoilt him and the cook overfed him. The little Princess Marigold loved him very much, but he soon grew so fat and lazy that he wouldn't play with her.

"That dog of mine is getting lazy and conceited," said the King to the Queen one day. "You mustn't spoil him, my dear. He will soon be so fat and lazy that he will expect us to run to him when he barks, instead of running to us when we whistle!"

Feefo heard what the King said, but instead of making up his mind to be better in future he growled to himself.

"Am I not the royal dog, the King's own pet?" he grunted to himself. "Why should I behave like ordinary common dogs, then? No, I shall lead my own life and do as I wish."

The next day Feefo felt rather cold, so he went into the Queen's bedroom, which was always nice and warm, and climbed into her cosy easy-chair. He spread himself out on the silk cushions and fell asleep.

When the Queen came in, she didn't see Feefo on the chair and she sat right down on him. "GR-r-r-r-r!" he growled, frightened out of his life.

"Oh, Feefo dear, I didn't see you," said the Queen. "I'm so sorry if I hurt you – but you shouldn't be in my chair, you know. I wanted to sit here."

But did Feefo move? He did not! He just lay there lazily, and looked at the Queen as if to tell her she must find another chair.

And then a curious thing happened to him. His tail changed from white to sooty black! The Queen looked at it in amazement, and then called the King.

"See what has happened to Feefo!" she cried. "His tail has suddenly turned black."

"Good gracious!" said the King. "What a strange thing! He must have been doing something horrid. The old witch who gave me Feefo said that he would remain as white as snow just so long as he was a good, faithful dog, putting his master and mistress first, but he would turn black as soon as he became selfish or unfaithful."

"Oh, Feefo!" said the Queen sadly. "I am ashamed of you. Go away and try to get your tail white again."

Feefo ran to the pond and held his tail in the water – but it wouldn't turn white.

"Well, well, never mind!" said Feefo to himself. "I'm a pixie dog, and if my tail is black and the rest of me is white, well, that's most uncommon. I'm sure *I* don't mind!"

So instead of turning over a new leaf,

the silly little dog tossed his head and ran back to the palace showing off his sooty black tail.

Next day the King wanted to go out walking and he whistled to Feefo. It was a cold day and Feefo was curled up in his basket by the fire. He didn't want to go out at all, so he pretented to be fast asleep. The King came and poked him with a stick, and made him get up.

"Feefo, you heard me calling you!" he said sternly. "Come at once."

Feefo growled softly to himself. He jumped out of his basket and followed the King out of the door. The wind was cold and Feefo was very cross.

"I shall slip back when my master isn't looking," he thought. So when the King met the Lord High Chamberlain, and began to talk to him, Feefo slunk away into the hedge and slipped off like a shadow back to the palace. Then he climbed into his warm basket again and went to sleep.

But, dear me, when he woke up, what

do you think! All his body, except his head, had turned sooty black to match his tail. Feefo caught sight of himself in the glass and stared in horror. He really did look strange.

"There!" said the King, when he saw him. "That is what comes of slinking away from your master, Feefo. What a dreadful-looking creature you are becoming, to be sure! Be careful, or I cannot own you as my dog any longer."

That frightened Feefo. For a day or two he tried to be the dog he used to be – but he had got into such bad habits that it was very difficult, and he soon disgraced himself once more.

"Feefo, come and look after the Princess Marigold for me for a few minutes," said the Queen, one morning. "She is in the garden. See that she doesn't get into any mischief."

Feefo ran out to find the Princess. She was bowling her hoop along the path and Feefo couldn't see that there was any need for him to watch her. He smelt a most exciting rabbit-smell under a bush, and decided to dig for the rabbit. So he started to scratch in the ground, and very soon he forgot all about the little Princess.

Suddenly he heard a scream, and poking his head out from the bush he saw that Marigold had tumbled into the fish-pond, trying to reach her hoop, which had rolled into it. The fish-pond was not deep, but quite deep enough to soak all Marigold's beautiful frilly clothes.

The Queen came running out in a great temper.

"Where's that horrid, disobedient, careless little dog?" she stormed. "Oh, there you are, Feefo! And what have you to say for yourself? But, dear me, this can't be Feefo! It's a little black dog, and Feefo at least had a white head."

"This last disobedience of his has turned him *all* black," said the King, coming up. "Well, Feefo, I am finished with you. You are not my dog any longer. I don't want a horrid little black mongrel. Go away from my land, please, and don't dare to come back again."

Feefo couldn't believe his ears. What, leave the palace, and the King and Queen, and go out into the world of boys and girls? Who would give him his dinner? Who would brush his silky coat? Who would stroke his soft ears and love him? Nobody!

"Did you hear what I said?" asked the King sternly. "I am not used to being disobeyed, Feefo. Perhaps you would like to have a good whipping before you go? I am sure you deserve it!"

With a long howl Feefo fled away. For a day and a night he ran along the high roads of Fairyland, and at last, as the sun was rising, he came to the great golden gates that led into our land.

Feefo slipped underneath them, and stood outside Fairyland for the first time in his life. Tears poured down his furry cheeks, for he knew what a lost dog he was! He really did love the King and Queen, and especially the little Princess.

He missed them all dreadfully, and longed to be back in the palace again.

But it was no use sighing and groaning. Feefo knew that he deserved his punishment. He set off once again, and began to look for a home.

But nobody wanted the strange little dog. Because he was a pixie dog there was something queer-looking about him, and nobody stroked him or petted him. They were really rather afraid of him.

Feefo found a little cave in a hillside and lived there. He lived on bones that the people of the village near by threw out. Soon he grew thin, for he missed his hot milk, biscuits, and nicely cooked chops. He was very lonely too, for nobody whistled him for walks, nobody threw sticks for him to fetch, and nobody let him put his nose into their hand.

"What a foolish dog I was to behave so badly to the King and Queen!" he thought a hundred times a day. "Oh, my dear master, I would walk a thousand miles a day with you now! And my dear mistress,

14

I would willingly lie on the cold step outside the palace door, if only I might be nearer you! And, dear little Marigold, I would never let you out of my sight, if only I had the honour of guarding you once again!"

Each day Feefo ran down to the village to smell out bones for his dinner. One day he saw a little boy sailing a ship on the pond. He had it on a string, and the little boat was sailing merrily along in the breeze.

Suddenly there came a strong gust and the string slipped out of the little boy's hand. The ship flew to the middle of the pond, hit a log floating there and turned over.

"Oh, my ship, my ship?" cried the little boy. "Oh, won't some one get it for me? Oh, what shall I do?"

He sat down on the bank and began to take off his shoes and stockings. He was a very little boy, and Feefo, who was watching, knew that the pond was deep. No one was near, and the little dog wondered what to do. He hated water – but never mind! He would be brave for once!

He ran to the pond, plunged into the water, and swam out to the ship. He took it into his mouth just as it was sinking and swam back to the little boy with it.

"Oh, you good, kind dog!" said the boy, hugging Feefo round the neck. "You *are* a dear! Thank you ever so much!"

Feefo was so pleased to find some one loving him again that he barked for joy and wagged his tail – and, dear me, what a very funny thing! He suddenly saw that it had turned white again!

"Ooh," thought Feefo, "if only all the rest of me had turned white too! I'd be a nice little dog again!"

But his head and body were still as sooty black as ever. Feefo ran off to his cave, pleased that he had helped the little boy.

Two days later, as he ran over the fields to the village, he heard the shepherd boy shouting loudly.

"Get away, get away! Wolf, wolf, wolf! Help!"

Feefo stopped and looked. Then he trembled all over, for he saw that a great wolf was crouching down beside the hedge, staring at two frightened lambs near by. The shepherd boy was afraid to go near, but the sheep-dog was barking loudly.

"Come and help!" he barked to Feefo. "This wolf is only a young one. We may frighten him away before he does any damage!"

Feefo felt so frightened that he could hardly get his legs to move. But just then the two little lambs bleated mournfully, and the little dog forgot his own fears.

He scampered up to the sheep-dog and began barking as loudly as he could. The wolf looked at the two dogs and bared its teeth. Then it suddenly turned tail and ran away.

The shepherd boy rushed up to the two dogs and hugged them both.

"You good fellows!" he said, "And as for you, little strange dog, you've as brave as any dog I've seen! You're not a sheep-dog, you're only a little chap, and I could see you were afraid of the wolf! And bless us all – what a peculiar thing – your body has changed from black to white whilst I have been talking to you! You must be a pixie dog!"

When Feefo heard what the shepherd boy said he barked with delight and ran to look at himself in the village pond. Sure enough, his body had turned white again. Only his head was black now.

"If only I could get my head white, I would go back to my master the King, and beg him to forgive me," thought Feefo. But for a long time he could see no chance of doing any one a good turn.

Then one night, as he was lying sleeping in his cave, a curious noise awoke him. He peered out of the cave and saw a row of horses and carriages going down the hill. They were very small, and glittered in the light of the moon. Feefo looked harder and suddenly saw that the horses were not horses – but rabbits.

"Why, it's a procession going to Fairy-land!" he thought, in the greatest excitement. "Yes, it's some great prince going to visit my King and Queen – but what's happened? Why are they calling and clapping their hands like that? They've all stopped on the hillside. I must go and see what is happening."

Feefo ran up to the procession of golden carriages. Then he saw what was the matter. One of the rabbits had gone lame and was being unharnessed. The courtiers were shouting and clapping their hands, calling for another rabbit to take its place. But none came.

"There are no rabbits on this hillside," said Feefo, running up to the courtiers and bowing his head to show that he knew his manners. "The farmers set so many traps that they have all left this hill."

"Good gracious!" said the courtiers. "Whatever shall we do? We *must* get to Fairyland before dawn. We have promised to take breakfast with the King and Queen in the morning."

The King and Queen! How Feefo longed to see them! Then a fine idea flashed into

19

his head. He would offer to take the place of the lame rabbit and draw the carriage. He would have to go right to the palace then, and perhaps he would get a glimpse of the King and Queen before he went back once more to his lonely cave.

"I'll take the lame rabbit's place," he told the courtiers.

"You!" they cried. "But you are a pixie dog, and far too grand to do rabbits' work."

"Oh, no, I'm not a bit too grand," said Feefo humbly. "I used to think I was, but now I know I'm not. I would be pleased to do this for you."

So the Prince was told and he agreed to let Feefo take the place of the lame rabbit. The little dog was harnessed to the carriage and off they all went once more. They soon came to the gates of Fairyland and Feefo barked for joy to see fairy folk again, as he galloped down the high road as fast as he could go.

And very fast he had to go too, for the rabbits scampered swiftly, pulling all the carriages smoothly along the road. Just as the breakfast gong rang out at the royal palace the procession drew up at the flight of steps leading up to the palace, and the Prince's trumpeter sounded his trumpet.

The King and Queen came to the carriage door to greet the Prince. The little Princess Marigold came dancing down the steps too – but the first thing *she* saw was Feefo – and do you know, he was *all* white, from head to foot! He had changed the colour of his head in his long gallop to Fairyland.

"Look!" cried Marigold. "There's Feefo! It *is* Feefo! He was black when he went, but he's come back white, just like he used to be. Oh, darling Feefo, I've missed you so!"

"That little dog kindly took the place of a lame rabbit, and drew one of my carriages here," said the Prince to the King.

"I'm going back to my cave at once, Your Majesty," said Feefo, rather afraid that the King would scold him for daring to appear at the palace again.

"Going back!" cried the King and Queen together. "Indeed you're not, Feefo! Why, you must be the good, unselfish, brave little dog you used to be, because you're all white again. We've missed you terribly. You shall stay here, and be our royal pet once more."

"Yes, you *shall*!" said Marigold, and she hugged him so that he almost choked. He was so happy that he nearly wagged his tail off.

He still lives at the palace, and if ever you go to visit there, you'll see him standing at the top of the flight of steps – and you'll be glad to know that from that day to this his coat has always been as white as snow.

2: *The Hidey-Hole*

Brian and Peggy lived in a very old house. It was called Old Priory, and their grandfather had lived there and his father before him. Daddy had often told them about his grandfather, their *great*-grandfather, who had lived there when he was as small as Brian and Peggy.

Great-grandfather's picture hung on the wall, and Daddy often said that Brian was very like him.

"He used to be like you, Brian, always collecting things!" said Daddy, laughing. "You collect butterflies, flowers and lots of other things, and your great-grandfather collected things too. All those old swords on the wall there are part of his collection

– and those funny old mugs in that cabinet."

Brian and Peggy loved their old house. It had funny little up-and-down steps from one room to another, the windows were all shapes, round, square or oblong, and the fireplaces were enormous.

And then one day Daddy said they would have to sell Old Priory and move to a smaller house.

"Oh, Daddy, why?" cried Brian and Peggy in dismay.

"Well, dears, times are very hard," said Daddy with a sigh. "I can't make enough money to keep up this big old house. It is always needing something done to it. Soon you will both have to go to good schools and I must save up for that."

"Couldn't you wait for a few years till I grow up and earn money?" asked Brian. "Then I could help to pay for the house, Daddy."

"I'm afraid I can't," said Daddy, smiling. "No, unless something unexpected happens we must sell the house this autumn, Brian."

Mummy was just as sad as the children. She loved the funny old house and lovely garden – but it wasn't a bit of use, they couldn't afford to live there much longer.

Brian and Peggy made the most of that last summer. They couldn't bear to think that soon they would be living in another house, a new house with no exciting old corners, no old attics where cobwebs stretched over forgotten chests, and no lovely gardens round it with the trees that their great-great-grandfather had planted – for he had lived there too!

Daddy bought a small house in a little town near by. The children hated the look of it after their own friendly home. Peggy cried about it when she was in bed at night.

"I feel as if my roots are being pulled up," she said to Brian. "We're like plants who have lived in one place all our lives and are being pulled up to be planted somewhere else."

"Well, lots of people do the same," said Brian. "Cheer up, Peggy. You'll soon have forgotten the Old Priory when once you've settled down in the new house."

"I never, never shall forget it!" said Peggy, fiercely. "And you won't either. You're only saying all this to comfort me – but you feel just the same as I do, inside yourself!"

"Yes, I do," said Brian. "Oh, I do wish something would happen so that Daddy needn't move after all!"

The weeks went by and Mother began to pack things into boxes. Brian and Peggy had to help and they were very sad.

"Mummy," Peggy said one day. "I suppose there aren't any secret rooms or secret cupboards in this house, are there?"

"I don't think so, darling," said Mummy. "Why?"

"Well, if there were, and we found them, we might find some treasure inside," said Peggy. "You know, Mummy – boxes of gold, or diamond necklaces, or things like that!"

Mummy laughed. "Oh, no, darling," she

said. "We shan't find any treasure like that."

"If we did, and it was worth a lot of money, Daddy could keep Old Priory and we needn't move," said Peggy.

"Things like that only happen in books," said Mummy. "They never happen in real life."

Peggy and Brian ran off to get some more things for Mummy to pack. Brian had been thinking of what Peggy had said.

"You know, Pegs," he said, "that's quite a good idea of yours, about secret cupboards and things. This is a very old house, and I'm sure that somewhere or other there must be hidey-holes. And if there are, there would certainly be treasure in them, because that's what they were used for."

"Well, Brian, shall we hunt for secret hidey-holes every single day till we have to move?" cried Peggy. "We *might* find something."

"Yes, let's," said Brian. So they began that very afternoon. How they hunted! First they went to the big attics and looked there. They pressed the wall all around to see if there were any secret doors. They hunted along the floor to see if there were hidden trap-doors. They peeped into the cupboards there to see if there was any chance of secret holes inside.

But not a thing could they find. They searched until it was dark, and at last had to give up.

"Well, I'm sure there are no hidey-holes in the attics," said Brian, sighing. "We've hunted everywhere. Aren't we dirty, Peggy? We want hot baths!"

"To-morrow we'll try the other rooms," said Peggy, hopefully. "If only we could find *some*-thing!"

Day after day the two children hunted here, there and everywhere. Mummy couldn't think how it was that they made themselves so dirty.

Soon September came, and Brian and Peggy were quite in despair, for that was the month they were to leave Old Priory and move into the little new house.

"We've hunted *every*where!" said Brian.

"All except the nursery," said Peggy. "But we know that so well that it's impossible to find anything new there."

"Still, we might as well try it," said Brian. "Then we have searched every corner of the house!"

So they tried the nursery. They even took up the carpet and looked underneath it. They felt round all the cupboards. They pressed all the oak panels that ran round the walls – but nothing happened at all.

"I suppose there's nothing by the window-seat?" said Peggy.

All round one big bay window ran a wooden seat, and underneath the seat was a cupboard where the children kept their oldest toys. The new ones they kept in the toy-cupboard on the opposite side of the fireplace.

"We might as well look," said Brian. So they opened the door of the cupboard under the seat. They pulled out all their toys and felt round the cupboard.

"Peggy," said Brian suddenly, "doesn't

29

it seem to you that this end part of the cupboard near the fireplace isn't as big as it ought to be? It seems too short to me."

Peggy popped her head in and looked.

"Yes," she said. "It doesn't look quite right somehow. Let's get a torch."

So they got a torch, switched it on, and had a good look at the cupboard. It seemed to be much smaller at the fireplace end than at the other end, and Peggy couldn't make out why.

"There must be some reason," she said getting excited. "Let's feel about and see if we can find some catch or knob."

But they couldn't. The wood was quite flat. There was nothing to get hold of at all.

And then suddenly something happened! Peggy threw an old wooden brick into the end of the cupboard and with a grating sound the top part slid open and the surprised children saw a dark hole beyond!

"Brian! Look! That brick must have hit a catch or something, and part of the cupboard end has slid back. Oh, Brian, we've found a secret place at last!"

Brian went red with excitement. He held the torch near the hole, but could not see anything in it.

"I'll have to get right into the cupboard and put my arm into the hole," he said. "I can't reach it from here."

So he crawled into the cupboard and got as far up the narrow end as he could. Then he felt round the hole, and discovered that the sliding piece ran in a groove behind the next piece of wood, leaving a square hole about a foot high.

He put his hand into the hole – and there was something there!

"I've found something!" he cried excitedly to Peggy.

"Oh, what is it?" she begged. "Tell me, quick!"

"The hidey-hole isn't very big," said Brian, feeling all round it. "There are two things here – something that feels like a box, and something that feels like a book. I'll get them out in half a minute!"

"Wait! I'll get Mummy and Daddy!"

cried Peggy, trembling with joy. "They must share in this!"

She sped off to get them, and very soon came back with them behind her.

"What have you found, Brian?" asked Daddy. "Hand them out and let's see!"

Brian crawled out of the cupboard and put something down on the floor. Every one looked to see what he had found. There was a square wooden box with H.H.L. stamped on it, and an old book.

They opened the box – and Peggy could have cried with disappointment, for all it contained was – what do you think? Why, just a collection of sea-shells!

"Oh, Mummy, it's only shells!" said Peggy, blinking away the tears. "And I did think it would be treasure."

"And the book is only a silly collection of old stamps," said Brian, in disgust, opening it. "And it's not even filled – there are only about twelve pages with stamps on."

"Half a minute, Brian – let me have a look," said Daddy, in a queer voice, and took the book from Brian. He looked closely at the stamps, turning over each page. Then he looked up and his face was quite red and his eyes were shining.

"Well, children, I don't know – but I believe some of these old stamps are worth a great deal of money! They must have been collected when your great-grandfather was a boy. He probably started this little collection and put it away with the shells in that secret hidey-hole of his – and then didn't bother about them any more. You know I told you he always loved collecting things!"

"Oh, Daddy! Do you really think the stamps are worth a lot of money?" cried Brian, eagerly.

"I'm not going to say for certain until I've taken the book up to London and shown it to a man who knows all about stamps," said Daddy. "But I think I know enough about stamps to see that these are very valuable ones – very rare indeed!"

Oh, what excitement there was in Old Priory! How they laughed and talked!

Daddy and Mummy each crawled into the window-seat cupboard to look at the hidey-hole, which was quite empty now.

"It must have been my grandfather's little secret place," said Daddy. "Fancy you two finding it!"

"Well, we hunted just *every*where!" said Peggy. "That was the last place we thought of!"

The next day Daddy took the book of stamps up to London and when he came back he hadn't got it with him.

"Good news!" he cried. "All the stamps are worth money, and five of them are worth heaps and heaps of money! Hundreds of pounds! What do you think of that?"

"Oh, Daddy! Can we stay on at Old Priory?" asked the children, both together.

"I think so," said Daddy "I've left the stamps with a stamp expert, and he will tell me what they sell for in a few days' time. We must wait for that."

Very soon the news came – the stamps had been sold for a small fortune, and

Daddy needn't sell their own home, nor even think of it! What a wonderful piece of good luck it was!

"Three cheers for great-grandfather!" cried Brian, standing in front of the old picture, and waving his hand round his head. "Hip, hip, hurrah!"

And Peggy believes she saw the old man in the picture give a smile.

3: *The Two Red Indians*

"Let's play Red Indians," said Paul. "Come on, Mollie – I've got my Red Indian suit out. Get yours, too."

"Red Indians are silly," said Mollie. "It's only pretending. We never really capture enemies or do anything exciting."

"Well, we will to-day," said Paul. "We'll stalk a real, live person and not let him know it! Come on! It will be grand."

"All right," said Mollie, shutting her book. "I'll come."

Paul put on his Red Indian tunic and trousers, and his big feathered head-dress. Mollie dressed up in hers, too, and very soon they were ready.

The children went into the garden and peeped over the hedge at the bottom.

36

"Now we'll wait and see if someone strange comes by," said Paul, in a whisper. "They shall be our enemy, and we'll stalk them. If they see us, they've beaten us, but if we track them to where they're going without being seen, it's our victory, see?"

"All right," said Mollie. "Here's some-one!"

"No good! It's only the milk-boy," whispered Paul. "He's going next door."

"Well, here's someone else!" said Mollie. "Oh, bother! It's Mrs. Brown. She's only going to the farm, I'm sure, for eggs."

"Sh! Here comes a *real* stranger!" hissed Paul. "Look! Don't let him see you!"

Mollie peeped through the hedge. She saw a man she had never seen before. He was tall and thin, and his hat was pulled well forward over his face. His overcoat collar was turned up, and his hands were in his pockets.

"This would be a good enemy!" said Paul. "He looks horrid! Come on, let's stalk him! Don't let him see you, whatever you do!"

The man hurried on down the lane, and climbed over a stile that led into a field. Paul and Mollie followed him, keeping close to the hedge so that they could not be seen. The man crossed the field quickly and went into a small wood near by. The two children kept him in sight, and found it easy to hide in the wood. It was most exciting.

"It's just like *real* Red Indians, this!" whispered Paul, excitedly. "Oh, Mollie, wouldn't it be lovely if the man was a robber, or something!"

"He looks like one!" whispered back Mollie. "What a horrid face he has got! Can you see the scar all down his right hand, Paul? Look, he's lighting a cigarette – you can see the scar quite clearly."

The man had stopped behind a tree and had lighted a cigarette. He stood there for some time, peering between the trees, puffing away at his cigarette.

"What's he looking at?" whispered Mollie to Paul.

"He must be watching that big house over there – the Grange," said Paul. "I can just see it from here. Perhaps he's going to rob it!"

"Ooh! What a fine enemy he is!" whispered Mollie, pleased. "If he does any robbing we might be able to catch him. We *must* stay and watch him, Paul."

"All right," said Paul. "Ha, little does our enemy know that Chief Black-hawk and his squaw Red-squirrel are tracking him! I say, Mollie, is it getting near tea-time?"

"It is, nearly," said Molly, looking at her watch. "But we *can't* go, Paul – it's too exciting. Let's be late. If Mummy is cross, we'll tell her we couldn't leave the robber until we had seen what he was going to do."

"Look! He's sitting down!" whispered Paul. "He must be waiting for something. Bob down your head, Mollie. He might see your feathers."

The man looked all round him as he sat

down, and then drew out what looked like a map. He studied it very carefully, and Paul nudged Mollie.

"Perhaps it's a map of the Grange!" he whispered. "Perhaps he's looking to see the best way to get in. All the people are away, you know, except the caretaker and his wife!"

"Hush! There's some one coming through the wood!" said Mollie, crouching low. "Ooh! Look at our enemy, Paul. He's hiding, too!"

Sure enough the man had thrown himself down underneath a bush and was crouching there to see who went by. A man and a woman walked down the path talking.

"It's the caretaker and his wife!" said Paul. "Oh, Mollie! I'm sure the man was waiting for them to go out. He's going to rob the Grange!"

Mollie was trembling with excitement. It was just like being a real Red Indian to track an enemy like this and watch what he was doing.

As soon as the caretaker and his wife had gone, the man stood up and once more looked all round to make sure that he was not being watched. He didn't see the two Red Indians hiding behind a bramble bush, nor did he guess that two pair of shining eyes were watching his every movement.

"He's going to the Grange!" said Paul, clutching Mollie by the arm. "Come on! Follow carefully! If he sees us he might come after us and catch us!"

The children stalked their enemy well, hiding behind trees, bushes and hedges, and making not a single sound, not even treading on a dead twig that might crack and warn the man he was being followed. The man was very careful too. He kept well into the hedge, and took cover behind every patch of trees that lay between him and the old house that stood not far away.

Soon he was in the grounds. The children squeezed through the hedge, tearing their Indian tunics, but they had no time to think of that. Everything was much too exciting. The man crouched down behind a yew

41

hedge and walked stooping to the house. The children followed him, hidden on the other side of the thick hedge. Then Paul clutched Mollie in surprise.

"Look at him!' he whispered.

The man took a quick look round, and caught hold of a rain-pipe. In two seconds he was climbing up it like a monkey and had swung himself on to a balcony above. Then the children heard the breaking glass, and knew that their enemy had broken into the house.

"Mollie! You run home quickly and tell Mummy and I'll stay here and watch!" said Paul, pushing her. "Quick! Bring a policeman with you. Oh, Mollie, isn't it exciting!"

Mollie ran off, her knees shaking, and her heart thumping. A real live burglar, and she and Paul had stalked him and he didn't know it! Soon he would be caught.

She ran home all the way and burst into the kitchen where Mummy was cutting bread.

"Mollie! Why are you so late for tea?"

"Oh, Mummy, quick! We've stalked a burglar, and he's robbing the Grange," gasped Mollie. "Get a policeman, Paul says."

"Don't be silly, Mollie," said Mummy. "You really are naughty, both of you, to be so late."

"But, Mummy, it's true, it's true. We followed this man, and he climbed up a rain-pipe and broke a window. Paul's watching him till I get back."

Mummy stared at Mollie in surprise.

"Aren't you just pretending?" she asked.

"No, it's true. Oh, Mummy, do get a policeman, before the man gets away."

Mummy ran to the telephone and called the police station. In a minute or two she had told them Mollie's story.

"We'll be round in a second," said the inspector. And almost at once there was the sound of a car and three policemen jumped out of it and ran up to the front door where Mollie's mother was waiting for them. Mollie told her story, and they popped her into the car to finish it, whilst they drove off to the Grange. The little girl was so excited that she could hardly breathe.

But, oh, dear! They had nearly reached the old house when they saw a little figure by the road. It was Paul.

"Hie, hie!" he cried, when he saw Mollie. "He's escaped! You're too late!"

The police stopped the car and Paul climbed in beside Mollie.

"He came out of the front door with a big sack," said Paul. "And what do you think? There was a man on a motor-cycle waiting for him in the drive! The thief jumped on the pillion seat and they both went off like lightning!"

"Did you see the number?" asked the biggest policeman, taking out his note-book.

"Of course I did. I'm a Red Indian and Red Indians notice everything! The number was OP6186, and the motor-bike went along the London road."

"Come on!" cried the other policeman,

to the driver. "We'll give chase.... Hold tight, children!"

Oh, what fun! What a glorious adventure. Paul and Mollie held their breath as the police car swung along the road at a terrific pace. Up the London road they went, and after about ten minutes they spied a motor-bicycle in front. One of the policemen took out a pair of field-glasses and looked at the number.

"OP6186!" he cried.

"Hurrah!" cried every one. Then a policeman took out a queer-looking instrument and began to tap in it here and there. Mollie and Paul watched him.

"He's sending a wireless message to the next big town to tell the police there to barricade the road," said one of the policemen. "We shall have some fun soon."

Sure enough, just before the next town was reached, the police there had put a long ladder across the road and all traffic was stopped. The motor-bicycle was stopped too, and when the police car came up all the policemen jumped out, went to

the two thieves and caught hold of them.
They looked into the sack, and found all
sorts of stolen goods there. Very soon up
came a closed police-van, and the two
robbers were pushed into it.

"I suppose these are the men you
stalked?" said the biggest policeman to
Paul.

"Oh, yes! This one with the scarred hand
was the enemy we followed, and that one
was the one hidden in the drive with the
motor-bike," said Paul, proudly. "We were
good Red Indians, weren't we?"

"I should think you were!" said the
policeman, and took them back to the
car. Then they turned homewards once
again and the excitement was over.

But not *quite* over – for the next week a
large policeman arrived at Paul's house
with two enormous parcels for the children.

"With kind regards and many thanks
to Chief Black-hawk and his squaw Red-
squirrel from the grateful police," was
written on a card tied to the parcels.

Paul and Mollie undid them—and what

do you think was inside? One parcel was a lovely canoe that Paul could really get into and paddle across the pond, and the other was a big wigwam, a Red Indian tent with all sorts of things painted on it.

"Ooh!" cried Paul in delight. "Look at these things, Mummy! Shan't we be fine Red Indians now!"

"You certainly will – but you deserve your good luck!" said Mummy. And they did, didn't they?

4: *The Three Strange Keys*

Once upon a time, in the middle of a dim wood, there rose a tall tower of blue stones. At the very top there was one little window, and at the very bottom there was one big door.

In this queer tower there dwelt a lovely prisoner. She was the Princess of Philomel, and old Dame Hoho had locked her in the Tower for six long months. She had sent word to the King of Philomel that the Princess could be freed only if he would give her twenty sacks of gold.

But the King was poor and he couldn't. He was dreadfully worried, and he didn't know what to do. At last he sent for a clever wizard and begged him to tell him how he might rescue the Princess from the Tower.

The wizard took a yellow bowl and put into it some strange things which he stirred together with a peacock's feather. Then when smoke began to rise from the bowl he laid down the feather and peered into the misty bowl.

After a while he looked up.

"Your Majesty," he said, "your daughter must be rescued by some one with three large keys, one red, one brown and one grey."

"But where can I find this some one?" asked the King, puzzled.

"That I cannot tell you," said the wizard, emptying his bowl and wrapping it up carefully. "You must send out a proclamation and see if any one comes along with the right keys."

So the King sent messengers throughout his kingdom, and every one hunted for large red, brown and grey keys.

Then one by one came princes, nobles, shopboys and peasants with keys of all sorts and kinds. There were old keys, so old that they had no colour at all, and had been freshly painted red, brown and grey. There were brand new keys. There were keys that were neither new nor old, but had been put away and forgotten.

The King looked at each of the keys.

"You had better all come with me to the Tower of Blue Stones," he said. "Then we can try the keys one by one."

So off they all started, the King in his second-best carriage, and the princes and peasants on horseback or on foot.

At last they arrived at the Tower. The Princess peeped out of the high window, and waved to her father. No ladder was tall enough to reach her, and she was very tired of being imprisoned for so many months.

"We've got lots of keys!" cried His Majesty. "Cheer up, my dear, you will soon be rescued."

"Which of us shall try his keys first?" asked a very proud-looking prince on a big black horse.

"Oh, you, if you like," said the King. So the Prince rode up to the Tower, and sprang lightly off his horse. Then he went up the steps that led to the big strong door.

Suddenly he turned round with a most astonished face and three keys still in his hand.

"What's the matter?" asked the King.

"Why, Your Majesty," stammered the Prince, in a surprised voice, "there isn't a keyhole in this door! So how can we use our keys?"

Wasn't that strange? He was quite right – there was no keyhole at all! There was no handle, no letter-box and no lock!

"*Well*," said the King, amazed. "Here's a funny thing! That wizard must have played me a trick! He certainly said that some one with three keys, one red, one brown and one grey, would be the only person able to rescue the Princess. And now we find that keys aren't any use at all!"

Back went every one, and talked about it till the King was tired to death of the word "keys". It was all very puzzling, and no one knew what to make of it.

"Well, I'll find another wizard and see what *he* says!" decided the King. So he sent for an enchanter and bade him use his magic to discover how to rescue the Princess.

This enchanter drew a circle around him in green chalk, and sat down in the middle of it. He set his cat beside him and then began to sing a curious magic song.

When he stopped, the cat opened her mouth and chanted a strange rhyme. This was what she said:

> A Key to give the witch a fright,
> A Key to scale the wall,
> A Key to carry a burden light
> Right over the palace wall!

"There you are!" said the enchanter, rubbing out the chalk circle. "Three keys again! I can't help you any further. Somebody with three strange keys has got to rescue your daughter, and it's no use any one else trying!"

Well, the King puzzled his head and so did the Queen, but nobody could make out what the cat meant. All sorts of plans were made to rescue the Princess but none of them was any good. The poor girl still lived at the top of the Tower and hoped one day to go back to the palace where her father and mother lived.

Now one day a travelling showman came to that country. He had two performing animals with him and a performing bird. He tried his best to please the townsfolk by setting his little brown monkey to dance and take round the hat, and by making his grey donkey show how clever he was at jumping over the skipping rope, and skipping up and down on all his four legs.

The performing bird was a big red turkey who wore a drum round his neck and beat it with his beak, saying "Gobble! Gobble! Gobble!" all the time, in a very deep voice.

But somehow or other nobody would look at the showman's animals and bird.

He got no money and was in a very bad way indeed. He had left a wife and three little children at home, and he didn't know what they would do if he had to go back to them without a penny in his pockets.

An old woman in a little village was sorry for the showman. She thought he looked very hungry so she gave him half a loaf of stale bread and a glass of milk.

"It's funny about the three keys, isn't it?" she said to him, as he stood eating the bread, throwing the crumbs to the turkey that said "Gobble! Gobble!"

"What keys?" asked the showman.

Then the old woman told him the story of the Princess in the Tower, and all about the three keys. She told him the rhyme, too, and he repeated it after her in wonder.

A Key to give the witch a fright,
   A Key to scale the wall,
A Key to carry a burden light
   Right over the palace wall!

"There's no sense in it," said the showman, munching the last piece of stale bread. "No sense at all. Well, old dame, thank you for the bread and the milk. I haven't taken a penny to-day, nor yesterday either. I shall have to go back home, there's no doubt of that, and sell my performing animals."

That night the showman slept in a ditch with his animals and bird close beside him. And in the middle of the night he woke up, remembering the queer rhyme that the old dame had told him.

"A red key, a brown key and a grey key!" he thought to himself. "What can it mean?"

And then, quite suddenly, an idea came to him, and he leapt to his feet. He disturbed his sleeping animals, and they awoke too.

"You're a red tur-*key*!" he shouted to the astonished turkey, who thought his master had gone quite mad.

"And you're a brown mon-*key*!" shouted the showman, pointing at the frightened monkey.

"And you're a grey don-*key*!" finished

the showman, dancing out of the ditch, pointing at the surprised donkey. "Yes – there you are, three large keys, one red, one brown and one grey!"

He jumped on the donkey's back, and bade him trot to the nearest town. The monkey jumped up beside him and the turkey flew up and sat on his shoulder. Off they all went.

In the early hours of the morning the showman arrived at the next town. He found out where the wood was in which the Tower of Blue Stones stood, and then galloped on the donkey towards the east, where lay the wood in which the Princess was imprisoned.

He arrived there just as night was falling. He could easily see the way to the Tower because so many people had tried to rescue the Princess that they had worn quite a path to it.

Round his waist the showman carried a long coil of rope, strong and thick. He undid this as soon as he reached the Tower. He whispered something to the red turkey, who at once went to stand near the door of the Tower. He whispered something to the brown monkey, who grinned and showed all his little white teeth.

And last of all whispered something to the fat grey donkey, who went and stood close against the wall, and made no sound at all.

The monkey leapt up on to the donkey's back, and then, light as a feather, climbed right up the wall of the Tower, carrying the rope with him.

Just as he reached the window at the top, a harsh voice below cried out angrily:

"Who's there? I'll turn you into black beetles!"

It was the witch! She was just coming through the wood to give the Princess her evening meal, and had caught sight of the showman by the wall.

In a trice he slid under a bush and hid himself, for he had no wish to be a black beetle. The witch thought her eyes had deceived her, and walked on to the door of the Tower. But standing there was the red turkey, and as soon as he saw the witch coming, he knew what to do. He spread out his big wings and rushed at her, crying: "Gobble! Gobble! Gobble!" at the top of his deep voice.

The witch thought he was going to gobble her up, and felt quite certain that the turkey was a magican. She gave a scream and ran away. She ran round the Tower, and the turkey ran after her.

"Gobble! Gobble! Gobble!" he cried. "Gobble! Gobble! Gobble!"

While all this was going on, the clever little monkey had managed to tie the rope to one of the iron bars across the window. Then he slid down the rope, and made way for his master.

The Princess had been most astonished at all the noise of "Gobble! Gobble! Gobble!" and was looking out of the window to see what was going on. But it was so dark that she could spy nothing.

The showman climbed up the rope till he got to the window. The Princess clutched at him and whispered:

"Have you come to save me?"

"Yes! Are you small enough to squeeze through these bars? I am too big to get in to fetch you. If you can get through them, I will take you on my back and climb down the rope with you. You look a very little thing!"

The Princess whispered that she could easily squeeze through the bars. In a minute she sat beside the showman on the sill. He took her on his broad back, and then began to descend the rope. The Princess was as light as a feather.

From down below came the "Gobble! Gobble! Gobble! Gobble!" of the turkey, still running after the witch. But suddenly they heard the door of the Tower slam, and the Princess cried out in fright.

"Quick! The witch has got into the Tower and when she finds I am gone, she will come after us! Let us get away as quickly as we can!"

The showman slithered down the last few feet of rope, and dropped on to the waiting donkey's back. The monkey leapt up in front and the turkey flew to his shoulder.

"Gee-up!" clicked the showman, and off they all went, the Princess sitting close behind them. The witch had found the Princess gone! In a trice she jumped on to the broomstick and sailed after them.

"Quick! Quick!" shouted the showman, and the donkey galloped even faster.

"Go to my father's palace!" begged the Princess. "We shall be safe there!"

The donkey galloped on and on. Behind them came the witch, lashing her broomstick to make it go faster still. She had nearly caught them up when the Princess cried out in delight:

"There's the palace! But, oh dear, the gates are shut, and the witch has nearly caught us. Can your donkey jump over the palace wall? Look, there it is, but it's very high!"

The showman looked, and called out something to the panting donkey. In a trice the clever creature rose into the air

and jumped right over the palace wall!
The Princess gave a shout of delight.

"Isn't he clever?"

"Well, he's used to skipping and jumping," said the showman proudly. "My goodness, that was a narrow escape, Princess. The old witch nearly got us!"

The Princess looked round. The witch was sailing round about the high wall, not daring to come any nearer. She shook her fist and then flew far away to the east.

"It's very late, isn't it?" said the Princess. "I expect every one's gone to bed."

They had – but they soon got up when they heard the great news. It went round the palace like lightning – "The Princess is back again!"

The King and Queen hugged and kissed their lovely daughter, and the showman stood proudly by with his red turkey, brown monkey and grey donkey.

"To-morrow, in the Great Hall, you shall tell us your story," said the King. "But now we must all go back to bed!"

So to bed they went, and the Princess was so pleased to sleep once more in her pretty silver bed with its blue coverlet. In the morning, what a crowd there was in the Great Hall!

"Tell us your story," said the King, to the showman. And he told it.

"I heard the rhyme of the three keys," he said. "A key to give the witch a fright – here it is, my big red tur-*key*, who said 'Gobble! Gobble! Gobble!' and frightened the witch almost out of her skin!

"Then here's the key that scaled the wall – my brown mon-*key*. He climbed up the Tower wall with a rope. And here's the key that carried the burden light and jumped right over the palace wall – my fat grey don-*key*!"

"Hip, hip, hurrah!" cried every one. "Hip, hip, hurrah!"

"What reward do you ask?" said the King.

"Oh, Your Majesty, I ask no reward," said the showman. "I am only a poor travelling showman with three performing animals, but now that they have rescued the Princess I think that every one will be pleased to see them perform, and I shall make a great deal of money. I ask for no other reward but that."

"Very well," said the King, smiling. "And you shall give your very first performance here in the palace. Such clever animals as yours are worth seeing."

The showman was delighted, and so were the donkey, monkey and turkey, who were very fond of their master. They did their very best to amuse the King and Queen, and when the performance was over, how they were cheered and clapped!

The turkey was given a bag of silver and so were the monkey and the donkey. The showman had a bag of gold. Then he and his animals and bird set off round the country once more, and this time, as you will guess, everyone crowded to see them. The hat that the monkey took round was filled every time, and soon the showman was very rich.

"We'll go back home now," he said to

his pets. "The turkey shall have a fine new drum. The monkey shall have a banana every day. The donkey shall have a saddle adorned with gold. What do you say to that?"

"Gobble! Gobble! Gobble!" said the turkey.

"Chatter! Chitter! Chatter!" said the monkey.

"Hee-haw! Hee-haw! Hee-haw!" brayed the donkey. And back home to their master's wife and three little children went – the three strange KEYS!

5: *The Goblin Chair*

On the top of Blowaway Hill was a little tumble-down cottage. It belonged to Dame Hush-a-bye, who had been nurse to lots and lots of children. Two of the children she had nursed lived not very far away, at the bottom of the hill.

They were Ronnie and Jennifer, and they used to visit their old nurse once every week, on a Thursday afternoon. She always had a chocolate cake for them and some ginger jam. They loved going to see her because she had such a lot of queer things in her little cottage.

She had a little glass ball, and right in the very middle of it was a tiny house. When Jennifer shook the ball a snow-storm came inside it, and flakes of snow fell all around the little house. It was a lovely thing to look at.

Then there was a little red box with a tight lid. When you opened it, there was another box inside, a bright green one. When you opened that, there was a third box, a yellow one. You could go on opening smaller and smaller boxes until at last there was such a tiny one that it was too small to be opened.

The thing that Jennifer and Ronnie liked the best of all was the goblin chair. It stood in a corner of the kitchen, the funniest little chair you ever saw. It was made of green wood, and each of the legs had feet on the ends, with goblin shoes on. The arms had hands at the end of them, and the back of the chair was carved like a face.

Jennifer and Ronnie begged Nurse Hush-a-bye to let them sit on this goblin chair, but she never would say yes.

"No, no," she said, shaking her head. "That chair's a funny one. There's no knowing what it might do. My great-grandmother got it from a goblin, but he told her she must only use it for ornament, not to sit on. So you be careful, and don't go too near, Ronnie. And whatever you do, don't sit on it."

Now one afternoon the two children arrived at Dame Hush-a-bye's rather early, and she was nowhere to be seen. They pushed the door of the cottage and peeped in. No nurse was there at all!

"Perhaps she's gone to buy the chocolate cake and isn't back yet," said Jennifer. "Come on, Ronnie, let's go in and play with those little boxes."

The children took the red box down from the mantelpiece and opened the lid. Just then they heard a loud sneeze, and they looked round in surprise. There was no one in the room at all!

"Well, who could have sneezed?" said Ronnie in astonishment.

"A-tishoo!" the children heard once more – and can you guess who it was sneezing? It was the goblin chair!

"Well!" cried Ronnie, in the greatest

surprise. "Who ever heard of a chair sneezing before?"

"It's your fault that I'm sneezing," said the chair, in a cross voice. "Why don't you shut the door after you? I'm in a draught."

Jennifer shut the door, and then the two children stood and stared at the surprising chair.

"Do you think we might sit on it, just for a treat, before Nurse Hush-a-bye comes back?" whispered Ronnie to Jennifer. She nodded her head. Ronnie went to the goblin chair and suddenly sat down in it. He jerked himself up and down on the springy seat.

"It's lovely and soft!" he cried. "Fancy, I'm sitting down in a goblin chair, one that has sneezed out loud!"

"Let *me* try!" said Jennifer – but, oh dear me, she didn't have a chance. What do you think that goblin chair did? Why, it suddenly put its arms round Ronnie's waist and held him tightly. Then it raised itself on its green toes, rushed to the door, flung it open and ran down the hill at top speed!

"Help! Help!" cried Ronnie, in a terrible fright, struggling to get off the chair. But the arms held him so tightly that he could hardly move. Jennifer screamed loudly, and ran after the chair.

"Ronnie! Ronnie! Jump off, jump off!"

But Ronnie couldn't. The chair tore on down the hill with Jennifer running as hard as she could after it.

The chair disappeared into a thick wood at the bottom of the hill. Jennifer ran into the wood too, but, oh dear, she couldn't see at all where the chair had gone. There was no path, and soon she was quite lost.

She was very unhappy, and she sat down and cried. Presently a big sandy rabbit came by and stopped at the sight of her. then he ran up to her and gently touched her arm. He looked at her with big, kind eyes, and Jennifer knew he was trying to ask her what was the matter.

"A goblin chair has taken my brother

away," she said. "Have you seen it anywhere?"

The rabbit shook its head, but slipped its paw through Jennifer's arm. He meant to stay with her, or go wherever she went. The little girl got up, and went on into the wood; she didn't feel quite so lost now that she had the rabbit for company.

Soon the two met a tiny man whose beard reached almost to the ground. When he saw Jennifer and the rabbit he stopped in surprise.

"Where are you going?" he asked. "Have you and the rabbit lost your way?"

"I don't know about the rabbit," said Jennifer. "but I've lost *my* way! I'm trying to find a goblin chair that has run away with my brother. You haven't seen it by any chance?"

"Well, yes, I have," said the little man. "I saw it not very far away from here. Come with me and I'll show you where. I'm a gnome, and I shall be only too pleased to help you, my dear. I'll come with you all the way, if you like. This isn't a very nice wood for you to be alone in, even with a big rabbit for company."

So Jennifer took his hand and he led her to where he had seen the goblin chair. Jennifer was quite sure that Ronnie must have been taken that way because she suddenly saw his handkerchief lying on the grass near by. There was a narrow path running through the wood just there, and the little girl, the gnome and the rabbit went down it.

They hadn't gone very far before they met two large hedgehogs. They couldn't talk Jennifer's language, but the gnome soon made them understand what they wanted, and he turned to Jennifer with his face beaming.

"Yes, they've passed the goblin chair away back in the wood," he said. "It was sitting down on its four feet having a rest. It was still holding your brother very tightly. Come on, we'll find it before very long, and then if a gnome, a rabbit and two hedgehogs can't make a silly goblin

71

chair give up your brother, I'll eat my hat and my shoes too!"

On they went, the two hedgehogs walking behind, all their prickles bristling fiercely. They didn't meet any one else at all. After they had walked for quite a long time, and Jennifer was getting very tired, the gnome caught her hand and pointed.

Jennifer looked to see what he was pointing at, and she saw a little square house set under some trees. The house was all yellow, with yellow chimneys, yellow windows, yellow curtains and yellow flowers in the funny little garden.

"That's where the chair has gone to," whispered the gnome. "The yellow goblin lives there. He has a set of yellow chairs and tables in his bedroom and a set of green chairs and tables in his kitchen. I expect your chair has gone to join them. Let's creep up and peep in at the window."

They all crept up to one of the yellow windows and peeped inside. Jennifer could see everything quite plainly. She saw Ronnie still tightly held by the goblin chair, which was standing in front of a tall yellow goblin and talking hard – yes, *talking* and laughing, chattering nineteen to the dozen!

"Oh, Master, how pleased I am to see you again!" said the chair. "And see what I have brought you – a boy for a servant. You always wanted one, didn't you? I would have brought you one before, but nobody ever sat down in me. How glad I am to be home again! It is quite a hundred years since I went away!"

"Let me go, let me go, you wicked chair!" cried Ronnie, and he kicked against the chair's legs with all his might. The chair pinched him with its green fingers, and made him squeal.

"I shan't let you go until my master says so," said the chair. "Now stop kicking, and I'll stop pinching!"

Ronnie was very angry, but as the chair could pinch him much harder than he could kick it, he stopped kicking and looked at the goblin.

"So!" said the yellow goblin, pleased. "I

have a boy servant at last! Good! Hold him for a little while longer, chair, until I make a spell to keep him here in this cottage for ten years."

The chair held Ronnie more tightly. Jennifer, who was still peeping in at the window, began to cry very softly, because she was so sorry for poor Ronnie. The gnome dragged her away so that the goblin would not hear her.

"Don't worry," he whispered. "We'll rescue Ronnie. I have a good plan. This is what we will do. I am very strong, and as soon as the yellow goblin has gone to get the things ready for his spell, I will climb in through the window and fight the chair. I will pull the arms away from Ronnie and he will jump out and run to join you. The rabbit can wait just outside the window for him, and when he comes you and Ronnie must jump on his back and let him run to safety with you."

"But won't the chair run after us?" whispered Jennifer, drying her eyes.

"Yes – but the two hedgehogs can

prevent that!" said the gnome, proudly. "One shall stand in the doorway with his prickles all standing out, and the other can stand outside the window, and then, as soon as Ronnie has climbed out, the hedgehog can spread his prickles out to prevent the chair from going out that way. Oh, it's a wonderful plan!"

He ran off to tell the rabbit and the hedgehogs what to do. They nodded in excitement. The rabbit stood under the window with Jennifer. The gnome peeped in at the open door, waiting for the goblin to go and get the things for his spell. When he saw that the chair was alone with Ronnie, he ran in and began to fight it. The chair doubled up its fists and fought back.

Ronnie slipped out of the chair, and the gnome told him to run to the window. But, oh dear me, just as their plan seemed to be going very nicely, the chair knocked the brave gnome down on the floor, caught hold of Ronnie, who was climbing out of the window, and yelled for its master, the yellow goblin.

The goblin came tearing back from the other room. He took hold of the hedgehog at the door, and pulled him right inside. He next took hold of the hedgehog outside the window, and pulled *him* inside too, Then he caught sight of poor Jennifer.

In a trice he leapt out of the window, picked her up and took her into the kitchen too. Dear me, what a crowd there was! The yellow goblin, the goblin chair, Ronnie and Jennifer, the gnome, the rabbit and the two hedgehogs! The goblin laughed a nasty laugh and slammed the door.

"Ho!" he said, looking round at all the frightened children and animals. "This is very nice. So you thought you'd rescue Ronnie, did you? Well, you'll need some one to rescue *you* now! What a nice lot of servants I shall have!"

Jennifer began to cry. The big rabbit took a red handkerchief from somewhere about its person and mopped her eyes with it.

"Whatever shall we do?" sobbed Jennifer. "Oh, how I wish we were at home."

"Nothing can save you now," said the yellow goblin, rubbing his horny hands together. "You are all in my power."

Suddenly there came a loud knocking at the door. The yellow goblin turned pale.

"Who's there?" he asked.

"Dame Hush-a-bye!" said a cross voice. "You don't mean to say you're up to your tricks again, are you, goblin? Where's that goblin chair of mine. And who did it run away with this time? Open the door and let me in."

"Nurse Hush-a-bye! Nurse Hush-a-bye!" cried Jennifer, gladly. "Oh, do come in and save us! This horrid goblin has got us all prisoners here! The goblin chair ran away with poor Ronnie, and it's still holding him tight!"

Dame Hush-a-bye banged more loudly than ever on the door, and shouted to the goblin to let her in. He shivered and shook but didn't go near the door. The big rabbit at last ran bravely up and undid the bolt. Dame Hush-a-bye walked in and looked round. Jennifer ran to her and hugged her. In a few moments she had told her all that had happened.

Dame Hush-a-bye turned to the trembling goblin.

"Didn't my great-grandmother punish you for this very same thing?" she asked sternly.

"It's only a joke," stammered the frightened goblin. "I just meant to scare them, that's all, and then let them all go."

"Indeed?" said Dame Hush-a-bye, in a very scornful voice. "Well, I don't believe a word of it. Tell that chair to let Ronnie go. It shall come back with me, and you shall give me another chair, too, to match it."

"Oh, no!" cried the goblin. "That would only leave me with one real goblin chair of my own. The others are just ordinary chairs. Whoever heard of a goblin with

78

only one real goblin chair? Why, most of them have four!"

"I daresay," said Dame Hush-a-bye. "Well, you're lucky to be left with even one, a wicked goblin like you! and now, you'll have to apologize to this gnome for your unkindness, and you'll have to give this rabbit the biggest lettuce out of your garden. And you must say you are sorry to the two hedgehogs, or I will tell them to prick you."

The yellow goblin grew red with anger.

"What! Apologize to a miserable gnome!" he cried. "And give my nicest lettuce to a silly rabbit? And say I'm sorry to those stupid hedgehogs? Certainly not! You silly old Dame Hush-a-bye, I don't care what you say, I'm not going to say I'm sorry to any one! And what's more, if you're not careful, I'll turn you into a water-snail!"

Ronnie and Jennifer looked at Dame Hush-a-bye to see what she would do. She never allowed them to be rude to her, and when she had been their nurse she had once whipped Ronnie hard for being rude to the gardener.

"Dear me, so that's how you feel?" said Dame Hush-a-bye, rolling up her sleeves. "You naughty, rude, little goblin! What you want is a good smacking!"

Dame Hush-a-bye took up a big yellow slipper from the floor, and caught hold of the frightened goblin. Smack! Smack! Smack! How she smacked him, and how he howled and wriggled – and how everybody laughed to see him!

"There!" said Dame Hush-a-bye at last, putting her sleeves down again. "That's a good punishment for you – just the same as my great-grandmother gave you, so I've heard. Now, are you sorry you've been so naughty?"

The yellow goblin was very sorry. He begged the gnome's pardon, he gave the rabbit his biggest lettuce, and he said he was very, very sorry to the two smiling hedgehogs.

"Well, now we must go," said Dame Hush-a-bye to the two children. "Come along. Goodbye, everybody. Keep out of mischief, yellow goblin, or I'll be along again. Tell two chairs to come with us, goblin."

Two green chairs marched out of the door with Dame Hush-a-bye and the children. The goblin stood at the door and watched them go, with tears running down his face all the time.

Dame Hush-a-bye took Ronnie and Jennifer home through the wood, and very soon they came to the hill at the top of which was her little cottage. Both the children felt very hungry indeed, and wondered if their old nurse had got her usual chocolate cake and ginger jam for them. But how disappointed they were, when they arrived indoors, to find that there was only plain bread-and-butter!

"You can't have cake or jam to-day," said Nurse Hush-a bye. "I think you were very naughty to disobey me when I was out. I have told you often enough not to sit in that goblin chair. Really, you almost deserve a smacking, like that naughty goblin!"

"Oh, Nurse, darling, you're a dear to have rescued us!" cried Jennifer, flinging her arms round her neck. "We do love you so."

"And we're dreadfully sorry we disobeyed," said Ronnie. "And, anyhow, Nurse, you've got another fine goblin chair for nothing!"

"So I have," said Dame Hush-a-bye smiling. "Well, well – you're good children, really, and you've said you're sorry. So perhaps you shall have your chocolate cake and ginger jam after all!"

She fetched them from the cupboard, and the three of them made a very good tea. The two green goblin chairs stood at the table, looking on all the time – but you may be sure that nobody sat down on them!

6: *The Tale of Sammy Skittle*

Sammy Skittle and his neighbour Benny Button were most excited – and no wonder, because the King of Fairyland was coming to their village, and had promised to have tea with one of them.

"He'll send the servants to peep into our cottages, and he'll have tea in the one that's the cleanest and the prettiest!" said Sammy. "Oh, I do hope mine is!"

"And I hope *mine* is!" said Benny Button. "I shall make some new pink and yellow curtains and hang them up at the windows. They will look very pretty and gay."

What an excitement there was in the two cottages! How the brownies scrubbed, polished and cleaned! You could have eaten off the floor itself, it was so clean. As for the kettles and saucepans – you should have seen them! They winked and blinked in the sunshine, so well had Benny and Sammy polished them.

The day before the King's visit there was really nothing to choose between the two cottages. They were both so smart and gay, and even the little gardens in front were full of flowers, and the paths well weeded.

Now that night, the Bee-Woman's cottage, not far off, caught fire. Dear me, what a dreadful thing it was! It was built of wood, so it was burnt right down to the ground, although the poor Bee-Woman and her friends poured buckets and buckets of water on the flames, and tried their best to put them out.

The Bee-Woman had six children, three boys and three girls, and they were very sad when they saw everything burnt. They had been bundled out into the garden in their nightdresses, and not even a cot was saved. They had nowhere to sleep at all.

Benny Button and Sammy Skittle had done their best to put out the fire. When the cottage was burnt, the Bee-Woman began to cry, and she said: "Oh, Benny Button, be a kind Brownie and let us sleep in your cottage to-night."

Benny Button thought of the King's visit next day. He thought of his clean floors and shining saucepans. He felt he really *couldn't* spoil things just when the King himself was coming.

So he shook his head and looked solemn.

"I'm sorry," he said, "but the King's visiting me to-morrow, you know, and I can't have my house messed up by your family, even though I am very sorry for you. No, you must make yourselves comfortable in the barn over there for the night."

The poor Bee-Woman was most unhappy. It was a cold night and her children were miserable, hungry and frightened. She did not want to take them to the draughty barn. The only things that were warm and comfortable were her bees, tucked away in their hives. The Bee-Woman remembered all the honey she had given to Benny Button, and thought he was very unkind and ungrateful.

"Sammy Skittle will be sure to say the same," she thought, "so I shan't ask him for help. I must just take the children over to the barn and try to make them as cosy as possible."

So she gathered her children around her and sadly went across the lane towards the barn. But she hadn't got very far before she heard a voice calling her.

"Bee-Woman, Bee-Woman, where are you going?"

It was Sammy Skittle, hurrying after her with an armful of coats and shawls.

"I'm going to the barn for the night," said the Bee-Woman.

"Indeed you're not!" cried kind little Sammy Skittle. "You're all coming to my cottage. Hurry up and put these coats and shawls round you before you catch cold. I've got a fine fire in my kitchen and there's a big jug of hot cocoa and some buttered toast waiting for you."

"But – but – isn't the King coming to see you and Benny Button to-morrow?" said the Bee-Woman.

"Yes, but that can't be helped," said Sammy. "I couldn't possibly let you go to the barn. I and Benny Button will put you up for the night."

"But Benny won't," said the Bee-Woman sadly. "He says he's not going to have his nice clean cottage all messed up."

Sammy was so surprised to hear of Benny's unkindness that for a minute he couldn't say anything. "Dear me!" he thought. "Well, well! This means that Benny will certainly have the King to tea, and I shan't, for my cottage will surely be in a dreadful mess! Never mind, I'm sure I'm doing the right thing."

"Well, if Benny won't help to put you up for the night, I dare say I can squeeze you all in somewhere," he said at last. "Come along, everybody."

All the Bee-Woman's family trooped

into Sammy Skittle's front gate. Benny Button saw them, and rubbed his hands in glee. "Ha!" he said to himself, "what a mess Sammy's cottage will be in tomorrow! The King won't set foot inside the door!"

Sammy Skittle made every one sit down and then he poured out cups of hot cocoa and passed round the buttered toast. All the children chattered happily, for they were glad to be warm and comfortable again. Then Sammy and the Bee-Woman began to make up beds for them.

There were only two rooms in the cottage, so it was a tight squeeze. Sammy let the three boys have his bed, and he put some blankets on the sofa in the kitchen for the three little girls. The Bee-Woman sat up in Sammy's big arm-chair by the fire, and Sammy himself sat in his bedroom chair and dropped off to sleep there.

What a to-do there was in the morning, with six small children to wash and find clothes for! None of them had anything but their nightclothes, so Sammy pulled out all sorts of old clothes from his chest. The children put them on, and screamed with laughter to see how funny they looked. The Bee-Woman washed them all, and told them they must go barefoot until she could buy them more shoes, for none of Sammy's slippers fitted their tiny feet.

Then they had breakfast. Sammy had only six cups, six saucers, and six plates, so the eight of them had to share, and what fun they had! There was porridge and treacle, and hot coffee and the children thought it was a fine feast.

Just as they had finished, the Bee-Woman's sister arrived from the next village, in a great way because of the dreadful fire she had heard about. She brought with her some clothes for the little boys, but none for the little girls, because she had only boys at home, not girls.

"You must all come back with me," she said. "I have a big house and you shall live with me until your cottage is built up again. You cannot stay here with

Sammy Skittle, in his tiny cottage. He has been very kind."

"We will come as soon as we can," said the Bee-Woman. "I must really help Sammy to get his cottage clean again. Look what a mess we've made of it. And I must go and see to my bees before I leave, too. I shall not be ready until after dinner, sister."

"What about clothes for the little girls?" asked the sister. "They can't go about in those old clothes of Sammy's."

"Let's wear Sammy's curtains!" said one little girl, pointing to the pretty blue hangings at the windows. "They would make lovely dresses."

"Certainly not," said the Bee-Woman, shocked. "Whatever next? No, you must just wear the old things Sammy has given you, and never mind if people laugh at you for a day of two."

The little girl began to cry, and Sammy was sorry for her. "What does it matter about my nice new curtains now?" he thought. "The King won't call on *me*!

Yes, I'll take down my new curtains, and whilst the Bee-Woman is helping me to clean up a bit, her sister can quickly make some little frocks for the three girls."

So in a trice he took down the pretty blue curtains, and the little girls shouted for joy. Their aunt cut out three tiny frocks, and sat the girls down to sew them with her. They would be ready to wear by the afternoon.

Benny Button saw Sammy tearing down his curtains, and he was pleased. "Ha!" he thought, "what ugly bare windows! The King won't even look at Sammy's cottage!"

It took a long time to tidy up the cottage. There was the dinner to cook, too, The three boys were sent out into the garden to play, but dear me, they came running in out of a rain-shower and made the nice clean kitchen floor even dirtier than before!

"Never mind, never mind!" said Sammy, "It doesn't matter. I can clear up properly when you've gone. Be happy and comfortable while you're here."

Wasn't he a kind-hearted little fellow? The Bee-Woman thought he was the nicest brownie in the world, and she made up her mind then and there to send him a pot of honey each week.

They all had dinner, and then the little girls put on their new dresses. How sweet they looked! They were so happy, and they hugged Sammy till he really couldn't breathe.

At last they were all ready to go. The Bee-Woman's sister had ordered the old blue cab to fetch them all, and they squeezed into it. "Good-bye, good-bye!" they called, "and thank you so much. We'll see you again soon."

Sammy waved till they were out of sight. Then he went into his cottage again. What a mess there was to clear up! Clothes all over the place! The dinner things to wash up! The windows were bare, and he must get out his old faded curtains and put them up before night-time. Sammy sighed. It seemed lonely without all the children, and there was *such* a lot to do!

Benny Button next door was rubbing his hands together in glee. Hurray! Sammy had no chance now to have the King to tea! How jealous he would be to see the King's splendid golden carriage stop at Benny's gate! The King would step out, frown at the dirty cottage next door, and walk up to Benny, smiling to see how spick and span everything was.

"I must hurry up and change into my new silver suit," thought Benny Button. "How grand I shall be!"

Sammy, next door, hadn't bothered to change his suit. He just put a big apron round him, and began to sweep the floor. He kept his ears open for the King's carriage, because he meant to peep out and see His Majesty.

At four o'clock there came the sound of hoofs down the lane. Cloppitty-clop! Cloppitty-clop! Sammy went to the window and peeped out. Benny Button, next door, was in a great state of excitement, and flung his door wide open, standing there in his silver suit, all over smiles.

It was the King's carriage, drawn by eight white horses, each with a black star on his forehead. Cloppitty-clop! The coachman pulled up his horses, and the golden carriage stopped exactly opposite Sammy Skittle's gate! Yes, *Sammy Skittle's* gate, not Benny Button's! Benny beckoned to the coachman in horror and shouted to him to back a little to *his* gate, but the man took no notice.

And then Sammy and Benny saw a very peculiar thing – from the King's carriage peeped the faces of all the Bee-Woman's children! Yes, really! And as soon as the carriage stopped the door shot open and out all the children jumped. They held the door open for the King – and he walked straight up Sammy Skittle's garden path and knocked on the door – rat-tat-tat, just like that!

Sammy couldn't move for surprise. The King knocked again, and Sammy fled to open the door, forgetting to take off his apron, and nearly falling over the broom.

He bowed to the King, but to his enormous surprise the King took his hand and shook it hard.

"Sammy Skittle," he said, "you're a good sort! As I came along in my carriage I met an old blue cab that had broken down. I heard from the Bee-Woman, who was in it with her children, all about the great kindness you showed them last night, although you knew that by making your cottage in a mess I might not visit you."

"Oh, Your Majesty. Oh, Your Majesty!" stammered Sammy, not knowing what to say.

"And let me say this!" said the King, raising his voice so that it reached Benny's ears next door. "I am most ashamed of your neighbour, Benny Button, who wouldn't help a bit! *Most* ashamed! I shouldn't dream of going to tea with him! I shan't even look at him. And, Sammy, I have come to ask you to go back to the Palace to tea with *me* to-day because I am sure your cottage is too muddled up to have any *more* visitors. All the Bee-Woman's children are coming, too, We'll have a *fine* party!"

Well, what do you think of that? Did you ever hear such a surprising thing! Sammy felt so light-hearted that he flung off his apron, put on his cap the wrong way round and went down the path with the King – and the King was *arm-in-arm with him*! Well, well, well!

Benny Button was watching through a crack in the curtain. How he wept! How he howled! How he kicked himself for being unkind! But it wasn't a bit of good, the King didn't even *look* at his cottage. That was his punishment, and a very good one it was.

Sammy Skittle and the Bee-Woman's family had a great time at the Palace. The King played hide-and-seek and blind-man's-buff, and every one was sorry when the party was over.

"I will build you a nice new cottage," said the King to the happy Bee-Woman.

"And as for you, Sammy, just kneel down for a minute!"

Sammy knelt down in surprise, and the King struck him lightly on the shoulder with his sword.

"Rise, Sir Sammy Skittle!" he said. "You shall be a knight for your kindness to others!"

Sammy went home so happy that he nearly fell into the village pond. When he got to his cottage, what do you think? Some one had been in and tidied it all up! Everything was clean and shining, and all the old clothes had been neatly folded up and put away. Even the faded curtains had been taken out of their drawer and hung at the windows. There was nothing for Sammy to do.

Sammy was puzzled. Who had done it? Only one person – and that was Benny Button! But *could* Benny have done it? He was not generally so kind and thoughtful.

Sammy ran next door and knocked. Nobody answered. He opened the door and went in. Poor Benny! There he was by his fire, crying bitterly.

"Yes, I tidied up your cottage," he wept to Sammy. "You can't think how ashamed of myself I am. I had to do something to make up for my unkindness. Do you think the King will ever forgive me? Oh, Sammy, what a horrid fellow I am!"

Sammy was kind. He comforted him.

"If you really are sorry, that's all that matters," he said. "I will still be friends with you, Benny, so cheer up. Perhaps one day you will be *Sir* Benny Button, just as I am *Sir* Sammy Skittle! But you'll have to try very hard!"

Off Sammy went to bed, and all the night he dreamed of how the King had knighted him – but he really did deserve his happiness, didn't he?

7: *The Noah's Ark Puppy*

Wilfrid's birthday was the next day and Uncle Dan was going to take him to the toy-shop to buy a nice present.

"You haven't a Noah's Ark, Wilfrid," said Uncle Dan. "I think I shall buy you one. Wouldn't you like that?"

Wilfrid didn't *really* want an ark. You see, he had a toy farm with dozens of animals so he really thought he had enough animals. Besides, he badly wanted something else.

But he didn't like to say what he wanted. So he just said, "Yes, Uncle."

"You don't seem very excited about a Noah's Ark," said Uncle Dan. "I thought you liked animals."

"Yes, I do," said Wilfrid. "But it's

live animals I like much better than toy ones!"

"Well, we'll see what sort of things they've got at the shop," said Uncle Dan. "Perhaps you'd like an engine better than an ark."

When they arrived at the shop, they went inside. It was a lovely shop. Balloons hung everywhere, kites and trains, dolls and golliwogs were all about, and, right in the very middle was – what do you think? Yes, a big Noah's Ark!

"There!" said Uncle Dan, going up to it. "That's just the kind of ark I meant, Wilfrid. Look at all the animals inside."

Wilfrid was just looking when he felt something licking his leg. He looked down and saw the dearest, fattest, brownest little puppy he had ever seen! It had seen Wilfrid and had liked the look of him. So it had run up to lick him, hoping that the little boy would pat him.

"Oh, what a darling little puppy!" cried Wilfrid, lifting him up and hugging him.

"How I'd love to have him for my birthday!"

"He's for sale," said the shop-woman. "He costs twenty-one shillings – just the same price as the Noah's Ark!"

Wilfrid looked at Uncle Dan, hoping and hoping that he would say that he would buy the puppy instead of the ark – but Uncle Dan didn't. He wanted to buy the Noah's Ark.

He did buy it, and he paid the money for it. "Please send it round to-night," he said. "It's this little boy's birthday to-morrow."

Wilfrid put the puppy down feeling very sad. He would so much rather have had the little dog than the big ark. It was a lovely ark – but the puppy was alive and could play with him. None of the animals in the ark could play with him—he could only play with them.

"Dear little puppy!" he whispered. "I would like to have *you* for my birthday, not the ark. I would love you and play with you."

The puppy jumped up at Wilfrid and

licked him lovingly. He would like to have gone home with the little boy. He did want a nice master like Wilfrid.

Uncle Dan and Wilfrid said good morning to the shop-woman and went home. The puppy looked after them sadly.

"Well," said the shop-woman to him, "what a pity that little boy didn't have you! I've got to send this ark to him, instead of sending you – but I'd much rather have sent *you*, because I could see he wanted you badly!"

The puppy listened and wagged his tail. And all at once a wonderful idea came into his head. He went into a corner and sat down to think about it. He thought and thought, and the more he thought the more he liked the idea. But he couldn't do anything until the evening, so he just sat and tried to look good and patient.

When the shop was shut the shop-woman used to go and have her tea, and then pack up any parcels that were to be sent away. The puppy knew this. He waited until the shop-woman had locked the door and drawn down the blinds, and then he watched her go and sit down in the little room at the back and begin to eat a good tea.

You'll never guess what the puppy did next! He went to the Noah's Ark and tipped the lid up with his nose. Then one by one, very carefully so as not to spoil them, he took each of the wooden animals out in his mouth, and dropped them in a dark corner of the toy-shop!

At last the ark was empty. Then that surprising little pup jumped into the empty ark, jerked the lid down on top of him, and waited to be packed up and sent off to Wilfrid!

Whatever do you think of that?

Soon the shop-woman had finished her tea. She came bustling into the shop, and began to wrap up the toys to be delivered. Last of all she went to the Noah's Ark.

She had a very big piece of paper for it, because it was a big toy. She wrapped it right round the ark, and then took her ball of string. She twisted a long piece round the ark, and tied it tightly.

"This ark feels very heavy," she said to herself. "I suppose all the animals in it weigh a lot."

There was only *one* animal in it—but she didn't know that! The puppy crouched inside, hardly daring to breathe. At last the parcel was ready. A knock came at the shop door and the woman opened it. Outside stood the boy who took her parcels round for her.

"Take this one first," said the shop-woman, giving him the Noah's Ark. "It's for Master Wilfrid Harrison, at The Nook. Be careful with it, because it's a Noah's Ark."

"I say, isn't it heavy!" said the boy. "I'll put it on my barrow carefully, and deliver it first, just as you say."

He went off, trundling his barrow. The puppy inside the ark was most excited. He really was off to Wilfrid at last. Whatever would the little boy say when he opened the ark!

The parcel was delivered safely at the house and taken into the dining-room. Uncle Dan took of the string and paper, but he didn't bother to look inside the lid. He just left the ark on a little table – and the puppy nearly yelped with excitement at being in the little boy's home at last.

When the house was still, and every one was in bed, the puppy lifted up the lid of the ark, and took some breaths of fresh air. He thought it would be safe to jump out and stretch his legs. So out he leapt. There was a chair by the table and he jumped down on that and then to the floor. He sniffed round the chair that Wilfrid always sat in at meal-times, and wagged his little tail very hard indeed when he thought of Wilfrid's surprise the next morning.

After a while he got back into the ark and lay down. He fell asleep, and only woke up when he heard Annie the maid sweeping the room.

How excited he was when he heard Wilfrid singing upstairs as he got dressed!

"It's my birthday, birthday, birthday!" sang Wilfrid, happily, thinking of all the presents that would be waiting for him downstairs.

At last he was ready. Down he went to the dining-room and there, on a little table beside his chair, were all his presents! You should have seen them! A big engine, a kite, two story books, a set of Red Indian things, three fine coloured handkerchiefs with his name in each corner – and, of course, the big Noah's Ark!

Wilfrid looked at all his presents in delight—but do you know, the puppy couldn't wait for him to lift up the lid of the ark! It suddenly jerked it up with its little black nose, and poked its brown head out with a happy bark, that meant "Many happy returns, Wilfrid!"

You should have seen Wilfrid's face! He was so delighted that he couldn't say a word! The puppy inside his ark – what a perfectly splendid, glorious, wonderful surprise!

"Oh, oh, oh!" cried the little boy at last,

and he lifted the puppy out of the ark and danced all round the room with him. "A real live puppy to play with! Oh, this is the loveliest present of all!"

His mother, his daddy and his uncle were just as surprised as he was. None of them thought that there had been anything in the ark but wooden animals. They couldn't *think* how the puppy had got there!

"Oh, Uncle Dan!" said Wilfrid, stopping in front of his uncle, and giving him a warm kiss. "Oh, Uncle Dan! You're just the kindest uncle in the world to think of giving me this puppy after all! I didn't want the ark! I wanted the puppy – and I thought you had really bought the ark with its wooden animals. I didn't *dream* you had told the shop-woman to put the puppy inside to give me this wonderful surprise!"

"Well, Wilfrid," said Uncle Dan slowly, "I can't understand it. I *did* buy the ark, *and* its wooden animals. I didn't buy the puppy. I don't know how it got there."

"Oh, Uncle! Didn't you really buy the puppy for me?" said Wilfrid, going quite pale with fear that he would have to give up the little animal. "Well, how did it get here, then? And where are all the wooden animals? The ark is empty."

"It's a mystery," said Daddy, "A real mystery. We'll go round to the toy-shop after breakfast and find out what's happened. But come along now and eat your breakfast, Wilfrid."

"I can't eat *any* breakfast if I've got to take my puppy back to the shop!" said Wilfrid, the tears in his eyes. "It *is* my puppy! It knows it's my puppy! Feel how it licks me!"

"Wilfrid, Wilfrid, you musn't cry on your birthday!" said his mother, wiping his eyes quickly. "That's very unlucky. You must be happy every minute."

"Look here, old son," said Uncle Dan, "you can keep the puppy, of course. If I'd known you wanted it so much more than the ark I would have bought it for you. But you didn't tell me. Well, you've got it now, and since you like it so much of course I'll buy it for you. The ark can go back to the shop."

"Well, the puppy's just the same money as you paid for the Ark, Uncle, so you won't have to pay the shop-woman any more at all!" said Wilfrid, dancing round the room again in joy. "Oh, puppy, puppy, you're really mine! Uncle Dan says I can have you!"

"Wuff, wuff, wuffy, wuff!" barked the puppy in the greatest excitement and joy. "Wuff, wuff!"

"Now, Wilfrid, you really must come and eat your breakfast," said Mummy, laughing. "It's all cold."

"Oh, I could eat twenty breakfasts now that I know I've got a real, live puppy of my own!" cried Wilfrid, and he sat down at once. The puppy had a plate of bread-and-milk, and in between its lapping it licked Wilfrid's legs until they were all wet. That was its way of kissing. Wilfrid didn't mind. He loved it.

After breakfast Uncle Dan went to the

toy-shop with Wilfrid. They took with them the ark, and the puppy followed on a string.

The shop-woman greeted them eagerly.

"Good morning," she said. "Oh, dear me, you've got the puppy! I thought it was lost! and do you know, I found all the wooden animals out of the ark in a corner of the shop this morning. Well, I can't think how they got there, and I'm terribly sorry about it, but..."

"*We* know all about it," said Uncle Dan, smiling. "This scamp of a puppy must have taken them all out, and got into the ark himself! That's where we found him this morning!"

"Well, did you ever hear such a thing!" cried the shop-woman in wonder. "I knew he was a clever little thing – but to do that! He must have wanted to belong to Master Wilfrid!"

"Wuff, wuff, wuffy, wuff!" cried the puppy, and licked Wilfrid's bare leg again. He was so excited and happy.

"I have a nice little red collar and lead

here," said the shop-woman. "I'd like to give it to the little boy for his birthday, to make up for the muddle that was made. I suppose you *are* going to keep the puppy, as you've brought back the ark?"

"Oh, yes!" cried Wilfrid. "The puppy's mine. I don't want the ark. And thank you VERY much indeed for the collar and lead."

The shop-woman brought them, and put the collar on the puppy. He did feel a big dog then! It was a nice collar, and the red lead was very smart. You should have seen Wilfrid walking out of the shop with the puppy on the lead! Dear me, weren't they grand!

Of course Wilfrid and the puppy are the very greatest friends, and they go everywhere together. And what do you think Wilfrid has called the puppy? I'll give you three guesses.... You're right first time – he's called him Noah, because he came out of the Ark!

MARVELLOUS ENID BLYTON

Enid Blyton could turn her hand to almost any form of writing. Did you know that for a long time she was the contributor on English fauna for the renowned Encyclopaedia Britannica? She wrote plays which were produced all over the world, poetry and hundreds of long and short stories.

In the Dragon series we have her two most celebrated stories about schools – Malory Towers and St. Clare's books, six volumes in each. Many children are so captivated by these stories, believing them to be based on fact, that they write in to us asking us how they can become pupils at these delightful schools. We have to inform them, regretfully, that Malory Towers and St. Clare's have no existence outside the imagination of their author.

Also in the Dragon series are the exciting "Mystery" stories, concerning the Five Find-Outers (and Buster the dog), not forgetting young 'Ern and Mr. Goon the village policeman. Thrilling stories – they have been read and enjoyed by millions of children around the world. If you haven't read them all, decide you are going to collect every one!

You should start your own Dragon library – a Dragon a week, and in such a short time you would have a collection of books to be proud of, gay in colour, bringing brightness to your room, and always there to bring you the pleasure of re-reading your old favourites. Why not determine to buy a Dragon book every week? They are still the finest value on the market.